A
Different
Boy

Paul JENNINGS

with illustrations by
Geoff KELLY

Old Barn
Books

AN OLD BARN BOOK
First published in Australia by Allen & Unwin in 2018
This edition published in the UK by Old Barn Books Ltd 2018

Old Barn Books Ltd
Warren Barn
West Sussex
RH20 1JW

Email: info@oldbarnbooks.com
Web: www.oldbarnbooks.com
Distributed in the UK by Bounce Sales & Marketing Ltd
Sales@bouncemarketing.co.uk

ISBN 9781910646465
Cover and text design by Sandra Nobes
Cover illustration by Geoff Kelly
Set in 12.5 pt Minion by Sandra Nobes
Printed in Denmark by Nørhaven

First UK edition
1 3 5 7 9 10 8 6 4 2

A Different Boy

Also by Paul Jennings

A Different Dog
ISBN 9781910646427

'The forest is dense and dark.
And the trail full of unexpected perils.
The dog can't move. The boy can't talk.
And you won't know why. Or where you are
going. You will put this story down
not wanting the journey to end.'

Praise for A Different Dog:

*'A tale of empathy, love, loss and friendship. A future classic
and compact story which will make your heart beat a little
faster and your eyes a lot wetter. Superb!'*
- @BookMonsterAlly

*'Full of quiet, resilience and graceful lyricism. Jennings' humour
peeks in at the end, gloriously.'* - @librarymice

*'A moving and powerful read for those looking for something a bit
different.'* - North Somerset Teacher's Book Award blog

*'Compelling and tersely written – every word counts – this is a book
to hold you in its thrall even after you've put it aside. Geoff Kelly's
black and white illustrations are atmospheric and powerful.'*
- Red Reading Hub review.

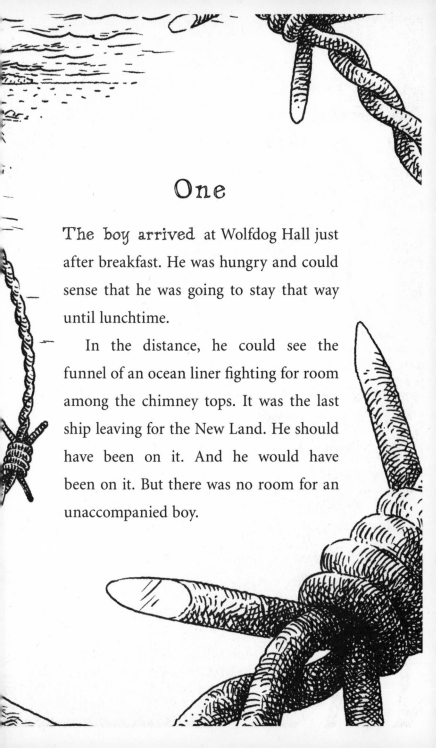

One

The boy arrived at Wolfdog Hall just after breakfast. He was hungry and could sense that he was going to stay that way until lunchtime.

In the distance, he could see the funnel of an ocean liner fighting for room among the chimney tops. It was the last ship leaving for the New Land. He should have been on it. And he would have been on it. But there was no room for an unaccompanied boy.

He was met by a bearded officer wearing a leather jacket with a large silver badge pinned on one side. He led the boy up the steps and through a gloomy entrance. The dark corridor inside was lined with thick wooden doors, each bearing the name and picture of a plant. Oak, Palm, Beech, Ivy and many more. The officer read them out in a loud voice.

'Here we are,' he said. 'Cactus.' He seemed to find that amusing. He took the boy inside and pointed at one of the six identical beds. Anton threw his pack on the bed and the officer immediately picked it up and started rummaging through it.

'Just checking for smokes,' he said. 'There are kids in here who would sell their grandmother for one. And other things.' He seemed disappointed that there were none to be found.

He pulled a small stack of labels out of his pocket and riffled through them.

'Here,' he said. 'O Muller. Pin it on. Just in case you forget who you are.'

He handed Anton the label.

'What's the O for?' said the boy.

'You get either O or C,' said the officer. 'O is for orphan.'

'What's C for?'

'Criminal.'

Anton's eyes widened and the man, seeing his expression, softened his tone just a little.

'Custody,' he said. 'The Cs have all been before the tribunal for robbery or assault or ... worse.'

'Worse?' said Anton.

The man scratched his beard. 'Don't worry,' he said. 'You'll be okay because you are an O. And the Os have privileges. They get to go out with relatives on weekends. If they have any.'

'I don't have any,' said Anton.

He could feel tears starting to well behind his eyes. He tried to blink them away.

'Well,' said the man, 'most likely you'll end up a C then.'

The boy looked puzzled.

The man sighed.

'It's like this. Let's say that a boy who is a C absconds – runs away – and he takes an O with him. The two runaways don't have anything to eat, so they steal. Then they're caught and brought before the tribunal and the O becomes a C.'

'That's not fair,' said Anton.

'Life isn't fair,' said the officer. He tapped his silver badge. 'Do you think I like this job?'

Anton felt a wave of despair wash through his body. He knew instinctively that he couldn't let it show.

'You and me could abscond together,' he said.

The man stopped and glared. Then, realising that it was a joke, he laughed roughly.

'I'll give you a tip,' he said. 'If you're thinking

of absconding, don't swim in the pool. There's so much chlorine in the water that anyone who spends any time in it will end up with faded yellow hair. It's the first thing the cops look for when an inmate absconds.'

Anton followed him back down the corridor and out onto a winding pavement. Two rows of boys were lined up. They were dressed in a motley mixture of grubby clothes. Jumpers, windcheaters and old jackets, most of which had grease marks from long-forgotten meals.

Each boy had a name label pinned on his chest. About half of them had faded hair.

Anton could already see scornful looks being thrown his way. A shiver ran down his spine. He was a new boy. It showed because he wore neat grey trousers and had fear written on his face.

The officer pointed to a space at the rear next to a thin boy who was shifting nervously from foot to foot.

'Stand next to Smit,' said the officer.

Smit gave Anton a tentative smile. Anton smiled back.

'Forward,' shouted the officer. 'No dawdling.'

The ragged group shuffled forward. A boy just in front of Smit opened a crumpled paper bag and took out half a biscuit. He shoved it in his mouth and threw the bag onto the ground.

'Pick up that rubbish, Brosnik,' yelled the officer.

A cold, sad memory suddenly swept through Anton as he remembered. His mother's voice. Saying that word.

'It's not rubbish,' she had said.

If only he could hear her say it again. Once the memory of that word had been painful but now that she was in a cold, cold grave he would give anything to hear her speak. He tried not to remember, but he couldn't help it.

He was only five at the time. He loved the way his mother read him stories. And he admired the way she could write letters and notes. So he had a try at writing himself. The old woman next door had come in to look after him.

He had grabbed the piece of paper and showed it to her. 'What does this say, Old Lady?' he said excitedly.

She glanced at his scribble and snorted just one word.

'Rubbish.'

He was so pleased. That night, when visitors came, he had showed them the paper and proudly told them that he could now read and write.

'It says "rubbish",' he said. 'Old Lady says so.'

They had all laughed loudly and he had run off to his bed crying. His mother followed.

'Don't cry, dear,' she said. 'It's not rubbish.'

That just made it worse, because he really thought he *had* written the word *rubbish*. He sobbed even louder. So, she took him on her knee and told him that he was sweet and that she loved him.

And of course he loved her – she was a wonderful mother. But the word *rubbish* always hurt. Now even more than ever.

Brosnik retrieved the offending paper bag and the line moved on. The thin boy next to Anton had the soles of one shoe flapping open like a slack jaw. He walked with difficulty, lifting his right knee high to prevent himself tripping. He suddenly stumbled and lurched into the boy in front who turned and barked his annoyance.

'Watch it, Skinny,' he growled. 'Or we'll fix your other boot too.'

'Sorry, Brosnik,' said Smit. He looked at Anton, trying to hide his shame.

For some reason Anton always made friends with boys who were shy or nervous or knew less than he did. He liked helping them. But he didn't know why.

'He's just a bully,' said Anton under his breath. 'Don't worry about it.'

He had spoken too loudly. Brosnik turned and spat straight into Anton's face. Then he shuffled on as if nothing had happened. Anton felt an urge to shove Brosnik in the back. But he thought better of it.

The procession wound its way through dozens of empty huts and reclaimed barracks. Occasionally they passed other men, all wearing the same uniform but not the silver badge. They nodded at the officer and he sometimes nodded back.

The school itself consisted of four box-shaped rooms arranged around a bitumen quadrangle.

Four young men stood in a row behind a short, older man who stood erect like a sergeant major on a parade ground. They were all dressed in suits, but only the older man's jacket looked pressed and neat.

The double row of boys stopped and turned to face him.

The officer pointed at the five men.

'Your teachers. The holidays are over,' he said. He was obviously pleased at the prospect. 'That's Mr Martens, the headmaster, and his staff. Do what they say.'

He started to walk away. Anton looked hopefully at the four teachers. Surely there was kindness somewhere in this place. Three of the teachers were hard to read but the fourth one smoked a cigarette and wore a casual, amused grin.

Mr Martens was a solid man. Now that the officer had gone he let his eyes pass slowly over every boy. He took his time. Finally he spoke.

'Okay,' he said. 'Now it's time for some hard work.'

A groan went up from the group.

'Yes, I know, I know. No more swimming pool and table tennis. No more lounging around.'

There were a few more groans.

'For those of you who are new, there are no locks on the gates here. If you want to abscond there is nothing to stop you. Plenty have. But they are always caught. Always.'

He let his eyes run across the group. He had a piercing, penetrating stare. He was in no hurry to speak. His silence said it all. Finally, he continued.

'For the benefit of the new boys, I will introduce my teachers. Boys aged seven and eight will be in Mr Hartog's class. He is also our music teacher.'

Mr Hartog shook his curly hair and gave a weak smile.

'Boys aged nine and ten will be in Mr John's class.'

Mr John nodded his head.

'Boys aged eleven and twelve will have Mr Hope for their teacher. You had better hope that you don't give him any trouble. Or you will answer to me.'

Mr Hope did not seem to appreciate the joke but he held up his hand in greeting.

Anton studied the faces of the teachers introduced so far. He realised that he had something in common with them. They were nervous. Perhaps this was also their first day. This was a tough place. Even for a teacher.

The headmaster cleared his throat and nodded as if he knew secret information.

'The older boys will be with Mr Steel. I know there will not be any trouble there.'

Mr Steel seemed not to hear. He threw down his cigarette and stamped on it. Then he gave a humourless grin and said, 'Otherwise known as The Claw.'

The older boys tittered nervously.

Anton guessed which teacher was to be his. He instinctively knew that all he would learn in that classroom was how to survive injustice and cruelty.

Mr Martens took a whistle from his pocket. 'When I blow this,' he said, 'you will follow your teacher. In silence.' He put the whistle to his lips and the boys sorted themselves into lines in front of their allocated teacher.

Mr Steel turned and nodded at an open door. There was a scuffle as his boys jostled through the door and raced for the back desks. Anton found himself looking at the last empty place, which was right at the front.

Mr Steel stood silently until they settled down. He waited a few more beats, then picked up a claw hammer and a large nail from his desk. He walked slowly across the room and began to bang the nail into the side of a cupboard. When he had finished, he opened the drawer of his desk, pulled out a long, black strap and hung it on the nail.

A soft intake of breath, mainly from the Os, swept across the room.

Mr Steel picked up a form from his desk and scanned it.

'Where's Muller?' he said.

Anton tentatively put up his hand.

'It says here that you're smart,' he said. 'You know plenty. But... you can't—'

'Swim,' Anton blurted out.

Mr Steel scowled at the interruption. Anton desperately tried to save himself.

'My mother drowned two months—'

'Yes, yes, yes,' growled Mr Steel. 'We all have our problems here. Some have dead mothers, some can't swim, some can't read, and some can't even wipe their own bum. So, I'm going to start you all off with something easy. In front of you is your workbook. You are going to look after it. You are going to be proud of it. You will never, ever lose it, abuse it or do anything but your best work in it.'

He glanced over at the strap hanging on the cupboard.

'You all have coloured pencils. You will spend the next half-hour decorating the front page. Make sure that it's neat. And clean. And you know what I mean by clean.'

Some of the boys sniggered.

'Yes,' he went on. 'No filth. No jokes. If I don't like your work you will do it again. At lunchtime.'

There were bemused looks and groans but Anton relaxed a little. He was good at art. And he knew a lot about it. He liked the work of Dali, which was weird, and also of the Impressionists, which was peaceful. He decided that an Impressionist style would be safe.

'Start,' said Mr Steel. He reached into his desk

and pulled out a newspaper and turned to the back page. He began to circle various items with a pen.

Each boy picked up a pencil. Some had their noses almost touching the paper. Some gnawed the ends of their pencils. Others chewed their fingernails. Some did nothing. Anton set to work. He began to draw a scene from the New Land. The place of his dreams. The place of his dead parents' dreams. A warm, sunburnt country – a land of sweeping plains and rugged mountains which ran down to golden beaches surrounded by a jewel sea.

The hint of a smile came to him as he worked. One day he would get there.

The boys scratched and scribbled in silence. Mr Steel sat at his desk staring at a book, not looking up even once. Finally, he growled, 'Stop work. Write your name on the cover of your book.' The boys began to scribble. Another thought occurred to him.

'For those of you who can't spell your own name, you can copy it from your label.'

At that very moment Anton felt a sharp pain in his arm. He gasped and turned around. It was Brosnik, who was sitting behind him. He had shoved the point of a pencil deep into Anton's soft skin. Anton pulled his arm away, knowing that he could not cry out.

Brosnik leaned over, grabbed Anton's book and plonked his own in its place.

Anton examined Brosnik's drawing. It was an unmistakable image of Mr Steel, with his pants down, bending over a chair. A smouldering cigarette was sticking out of his backside. Anton knew without even looking that his own name had been written on the cover of Brosnik's book.

Mr Steel looked at the class.

'Take up the books... Muller,' he said.

Anton stood and stared around the classroom. The awful truth dawned on him. The faces of all the boys showed fear, loneliness or anger. The teachers he had seen outside were mean or weak. There was no hope here. It was a place of despair.

If he handed in the rude drawing he would get the strap. And if he named Brosnik as the guilty party he would be in for a beating from the bullies. The other kids would be too frightened to support him even if they wanted to.

The words of his dead father came back to him. The words he had spoken when he surveyed the ruins of their bombed-out street.

'If you've got a bad deal,' his father had said, 'get out of it and move on.'

Anton slowly put Brosnik's book down on the desk and walked to the door.

'Where do you think you're going?' growled Mr Steel.

Anton opened the door.

'I'm getting out of it,' he said, 'and moving on.'

The other boys were staring at Anton with wide eyes. Some in disbelief, some in horror. Brosnik was grinning like a spectator at an execution.

Anton could hardly believe what he was doing himself. His strength was only just greater than his fear. But he took the final step and opened the door.

To his surprise, Mr Steel did not come after him. He did not yell. He merely walked over to the empty desk, picked up the book containing the drawing and glanced at the first page.

'You'll be back,' he said. 'And when you are you will be sorry.'

Anton shivered, stepped out of the classroom and walked into the deserted quadrangle. He hurried away between two of the portable classrooms. He tried to walk slowly, even though every muscle seemed to be willing him into a run.

He followed a footpath past a swimming pool. The smell of chlorine filled the air. A piece of wood dangled on the wire gate. It was a crude sign, with a red line slashed across the outline of a boy peeing into the pool.

He shuddered. He couldn't swim, but even if he could there was no chance he would have entered that pool. Ever.

He reached the boundary fence and passed out through a wire gate. A bitterly cold wind was blowing. His thick black hair whipped his eyes and made them water. But he hardly noticed it.

He was free.

But there was nowhere to go. His empty stomach rumbled. He had no money. No friends. He would probably end up returning to Wolfdog Hall just to get something to eat. Or he would have to steal food. The officer's words rang in his ears. Now he understood them.

'Most likely you'll end up a C.'

Anton was standing on the side of a grassy slope. In the distance, the grey sea was visible over the bombed-out rooftops. Smoke curled slowly up from the distant mountains where the fighting had been so fierce.

The clouds were grey and unfriendly and bore the threat of rain. He shivered inside his jumper.

A loud, deep horn sounded across the town. He could see the funnel of the ship etched against the sky. Maybe it was still tied to the pier.

He began walking down the hill.

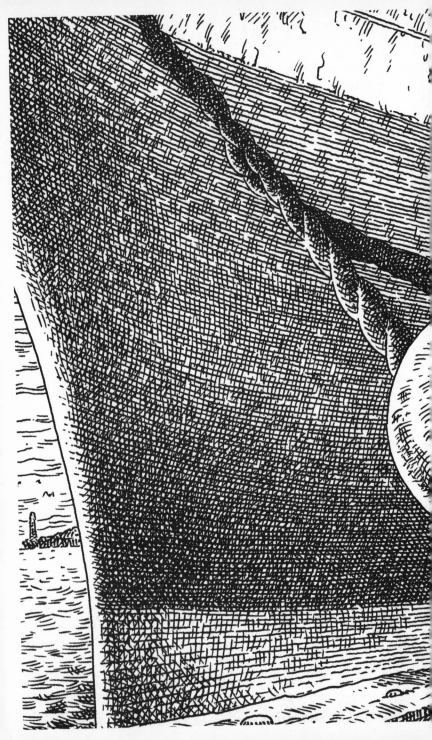

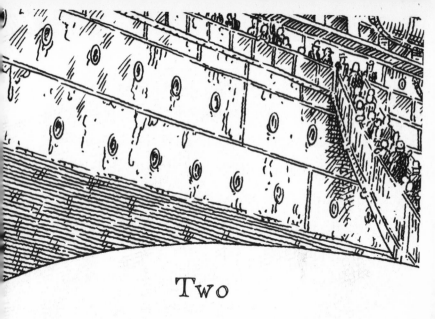

Two

The ship was a towering fortress. That's the way Anton thought about it. He had never even seen a building as big as the ocean liner that loomed over the pier. But he knew what it was and where it was going.

He stared enviously at the people lining up in front of the wide gangplank.

How he wished that he was one of the chosen ones. Heading off on a voyage to a land of peace and plenty. Leaving the land of broken buildings and crushed hopes behind. Looking forward to sunshine and steaks. To adventures in the forests and mountains. A place to grow and prosper.

Parents were herding their happy children onto the gangplank and on to the waiting deck above. A band played a tune to the huge crowd lining the pier. A sad, sweet melody of longing and hope. Teary relatives waved as they farewelled the lucky emigrants.

A blanket of sadness swept over Anton. Even if he had a place on the ship, there would be no one to remember him. There would be no tears or goodbyes. If he sailed away to the New Land, not one person would miss him. No one at Wolfdog Hall even knew his first name.

He stood there transfixed as the line of impatient travellers began to dwindle. Eventually, only a few stragglers were left waiting for the two uniformed officers to check their boarding passes. How Anton wished he was holding one of those magic pieces of paper.

A thin woman dressed from head to foot in black was one of those left to board. An impatient official was waiting for her to find something in the bottom of a bulging bag. A tall boy of about fourteen or fifteen was standing behind her.

The boy grinned at Anton with an over-generous smile and pulled his coloured beanie down over his ears.

'Don't go near the edge, Max,' the woman said without looking up.

The boy didn't seem to hear his mother. She called out over her shoulder.

'Stay there, Max.'

'Stay there, Max,' the grinning boy mumbled back. He wasn't really listening. He was staring at Anton.

One of the ship's crew was already loosening the gangplank ropes. He paid no attention to the boy or Anton.

There was something odd about this boy's face. It seemed unusually smooth. It reminded Anton of a porcelain doll's head, without a blemish or a wrinkle.

The boy's jumper was covered in ribbons, badges and labels – awards for everything from dog shows to athletic events. There were also buttons with pictures proclaiming dozens of causes. Anton smiled. The boy looked like a human noticeboard.

His smile faded when he saw that the boy was also wearing a black armband. It reminded Anton of the one he had been wearing himself only a few weeks ago.

Almost hidden among the clutter on the boy's chest were two brass medals, which Anton knew were awarded to brave soldiers who had died in battle.

The boy was grinning and nodding and pointing at Anton, who smiled in return.

'I'm Anton,' he said.

'I'm Anton,' said the boy.

'No, you're Max,' said Anton.

'You're Max,' said Max. He tapped Anton's chest with one finger.

'Ah, that's what you want,' said Anton. He unclipped the small safety pin and handed over his label. He smiled back as the boy clumsily pinned it on himself.

The boy began pointing to his own chest. 'Read, read, read,' he yelled excitedly.

'O Muller,' said Anton.

Anton looked at the boy's face for a response. But there was none. He suddenly realised the reason for the boy's porcelain appearance. He had no eyelashes. Or eyebrows. Anton guessed that under the beanie he had no hair either.

One of the sailors looked up. He was anxious to go.

'Are you two together?' he asked.

'Two together,' said Max.

The sailor nodded and turned back to his rope.

Max held out a hand and started to laugh crazily.

'Shake, shake, shake,' he yelled.

Anton took Max's hand and the boy pumped it up and down. They grinned at each other.

Max took a step towards the gangplank and, still hanging tightly on to Anton's hand, pulled him along behind.

Anton felt himself being led up the gangplank. He followed like a small child. He could not believe that he was allowing this to happen. He was boarding the ship. Without a pass. His feet seemed to belong to someone else. They were taking him up towards the deck.

For a moment, he looked back across the streets, still littered with rubble from the war. It was dreary and dangerous. A land full of orphans and queues for food. And places with pools full of piss. It was a dangerous land. But it was all he knew. Bad as it was – it was home.

He looked up the gangplank. The boat beckoned. It might lead him to rugged mountain ranges and jewel seas. But what about droughts and flooding rains?

He was possessed by an overwhelming sense that something huge was happening. That if he took another step, nothing would ever be the same again. He hesitated.

And took another step.

He followed Max up onto the deck where the boy's mother was waiting. She wore a sad expression but seemed pleased to see them arrive hand in hand.

'You've found a friend, Max,' she said. 'That's lovely…' She shouted something else but it was drowned out by a mournful growl from the ship's funnel.

The railings were lined with waving people. Pleased that they had reached the top of the long waiting list and held tickets to better place. Unhappy that their loved ones were not able to follow. Those sailing and those staying all knew the same thing. The ship held six hundred people. It was the last voyage and the people left behind would stay behind.

The deck was crowded and there was much jostling as the emigrants sought one last glimpse of their loved ones. Ropes were released. The gangplank withdrawn. A deep-throated *whoop, whoop* filled the air. Tugs pushed and churned.

The band played on as an ever-widening river of sea emerged between the dock and the ship. It seemed to Anton that the people on the pier below were receding into the past like sad memories. The tugs departed and the ship's propellers began to thrash and bite into the water. Finally, the farewelling crowd faded altogether and the pier became nothing but a thin line floating on the edge of the bay.

The passengers began to desert the railings and go searching for their cabins. The excitement seemed to have drained into the grey sea as the emigrants accepted that they had left home forever – loss made their good fortune hard to enjoy.

'New friend, new friend, new friend,' laughed Max.

His mother threw a questioning smile at Anton. 'Where are your parents?' she asked as she took Max's hand.

Anton tried to stop the fear showing itself on his face. He scrabbled unsuccessfully to find an answer. He stared at the numbers on the cabin doors behind her but they were of no use. He pointed at a row of doors further along the deck.

She looked surprised. 'Aren't you lucky. A deck-cabin.' She started to walk away but Max pulled back.

'Want friend, want friend, want friend,' he yelled.

'It's all right dear,' said Max's mother. 'He can visit whenever he likes.' Then she added, 'If his parents agree.'

'Parents agree,' said Max.

'We are in C 32,' she told Anton. 'In steerage.'

Anton smiled at Max. 'I'll see you later, Max,' he said.

'Later, Max,' the boy replied with a pout. Then he shouted, 'Don't go, don't go. Like boy. Like boy.'

Anton knew that he had to go. He also knew that he had nowhere to go.

He turned and hurried along the deck.

'Come and visit,' Max's mother called after him. 'My name is Pat.'

The crowd on the deck had gone and it was growing cold. A chill wind was blowing from the north. And the sun was sinking into a cold and unforgiving sea.

Three

The midwife was old. Her cheeks drooped like the jowls on a bulldog. Her manner was gruff but her face was kindly.

'Don't worry,' she said. 'I've done this before. Thousands of times.'

'Thousands?' said the woman.

'At least a hundred a year. For forty years. You work it out.'

'Twins?' said the expectant mother.

'I've brought dozens of twins into this world. Scores,' said the midwife.

The mother still looked disappointed. 'I was hoping for a …'

'Doctor,' said the midwife. 'I know. But the fighting took so many of…'

'It took my husband as well,' said the mother, 'and…' She gasped and held her swollen belly.

'They are coming,' she groaned.

And come they did.

* * *

The mother could tell by the midwife's expression that something was not quite right, but she held out her hands with an eager smile. The midwife placed one baby in each of her arms.

The mother peered at the little pink faces. She beamed at them and then said, 'Not identical?'

'Yes, identical but… different,' said the midwife.

The mother was puzzled. 'They've got no hair. But most babies are bald, aren't they?' she said.

'Hypotrichosis,' said the midwife. 'They won't have hair or eyebrows. Or eyelashes.'

'This one is smaller,' said the mother.

The midwife nodded. 'Usually twins have a separate supply of blood in the womb,' she said. 'But these shared an artery.'

'So?'

'So the big one got more of the blood. And more of the oxygen. Both boys will look the same when the little one catches up. But he may have problems.'

'What sort of problems?' said the mother.

'It's too early to say,' said the midwife. 'But there could be brain damage.'

The mother let this sink in as she gave a loving smile to the smaller twin. 'He might need special help,' she said. 'He's the same but different.'

'Special,' said the midwife.

'No,' said the mother. 'They are both special.'

Four

Anton stared at the choppy grey sea. Now that the wintry sun had dipped below the horizon he was cold. He shivered and leaned over the solid rail that ran around the ship. Far below, the waves reached up as the bow dug into a trough.

He looked around at the deserted deck. He had to find somewhere to hide. Somewhere warm.

The realisation began to sink in. He was a stowaway. If he was discovered he would be sent back to the orphanage. Maybe not right away, but at the first port.

There would be other migrant ships returning from the land of his dreams. They could put him on one of them. He would never get to the top of the waiting list. There was no waiting list.

He had heard stories about stowaways on sailing ships. Adventure, fun, pirates and buried gold. But this was the real world. A steel boat with empty decks and closed doors. With hatches and ladders so cold they could rip the skin off your fingers.

He was wearing only thin trousers, a shirt and his jumper. Salty spray was whipping his face. Down below there would be snug cabins and a dining room with regular meals. Families. Possibly a makeshift schoolroom and a sick bay.

The ship dug into another wave and his empty stomach heaved. He gagged and choked but nothing came. The dry-retching was worse than vomiting. There was no relief for his empty stomach.

A heavy hand suddenly fell on his shoulder.

'What are you doing here, lad?' said a voice. 'You shouldn't be on deck alone in this weather.'

He turned and saw a man wearing a thick woollen coat and a navy peaked cap.

'What's the number of your cabin, son?' he said. 'I'll take you back. And have a few words with your parents.'

Anton's head began to spin. Tears filled his eyes. He was caught. Already. On the first day. He didn't know what to say. Images flashed before him.

'What's the matter?' said the man. 'What is it?'

Anton fought for clarity but none came. He was so tired. Dreamlike images passed through his aching head.

'Sunshine and steaks,' he mumbled. He fought to dismiss the wandering thoughts as scraps of a poem flitted through his mind.

'Droughts and flooding rains. Ringbarked forests. A sunburnt country.'

The man shook his head and smiled. 'You'll get there soon enough,' he said. 'It only takes five weeks. But if you stay up here you might end up feeding the fishes.'

Anton looked puzzled.

'Washed overboard,' the man said grimly.

A large wave hit the side of the ship and lashed them with spray.

The man still held Anton's shoulder with a firm hand. He turned the boy like someone twisting a lid on a jar.

'This way,' he yelled. His words were snatched away by the roar of the sea.

He steered Anton across the deck and through a door. It closed behind them with a clang. They were in a large empty hallway with several doors on each side and a staircase leading down into the gloom.

'What's your name?' the man said.

The cold and the fear made it hard to think. He just told the truth.

'Anton.' He trembled.

'What's your cabin number?'

He searched his mind. But found only one answer.

'C 32,' he whispered. And then he added, 'In steerage.'

The man gave an amused grin. 'Come on then,' he said. He led Anton down the staircase and along a narrow corridor. It twisted and turned. Down another staircase. More gloomy corridors. Dim flickering lights. No windows.

The boy followed blindly, his head swimming with images and memories. It was like a waking dream. His father fighting in the never-ending war. His mother, dead in her coffin as they lowered it into the grave. The lady from the government giving him a handful of dirt to throw onto the lid. Staying in the foster home for a few days. And then, and then...Wolfdog Hall. The leather strap. A dozen leather straps. Labels and rude drawings. He began to shake uncontrollably.

'We're nearly there,' said the man.

Anton nodded wearily. He was so tired. Like a criminal being led to the gallows, he just wanted it to be over.

They stopped at a cabin door. C 32. The man rapped on it three times.

The door opened. Max's shining face stared out.

'Is your mother here?' said the man. 'This boy was alone on deck.'

'On deck,' repeated Max. 'Is Anton. Nice boy, nice boy, Anton,' he yelled. He jumped up and down and clapped his hands excitedly.

'He's with you then?' said the man.

'With you,' mumbled Max. He grabbed Anton's wrist and yanked him inside the cabin. Then he slammed the steel door in the face of the surprised man.

Anton stared around. The cabin was small and dark without a porthole. Against one wall was a small single bed. Opposite was a pair of bunks and a desk. On the desk was a photograph of two boys smiling at the camera with their arms around each other. It was Max and... Max again. Both of the boys were bald with smooth shiny faces. Before he could make sense of this he was distracted by the sound of water running. He guessed it was from a bathroom.

Max ran over to an open suitcase on the floor. He pulled out two glove puppets. Identical boy puppets with bald heads. Identical except for their small knitted jumpers. One was green and the other red. Max slipped his hand inside the red puppet and threw the green one at Anton. 'Talk, talk,' he yelled.

Anton sighed wearily. By now his stomach was settled and the gnawing hunger had returned. He looked at the bottom bunk. If only he could get under the blanket and close his eyes.

'Talk, talk,' shouted Max. He was becoming upset.

Anton threw a glance at the bathroom door. 'Shh,' he said. 'Shh …'

Max seemed not to hear. He opened and shut the lips of the red puppet.

'Talk, talk,' he shouted.

Anton threw another glance at the bathroom door and then at the empty bunk. He sighed. Then he sat down on the bunk and slipped his hand into the green puppet.

'Christopher,' said Max happily.

He started jabbing Anton with the red puppet. 'Talk, talk,' he yelled. 'Make Christopher talk.'

Anton used his thumb and forefinger to open the little mouth on the puppet. He spoke with his teeth clenched together in the manner of a ventriloquist.

'I have run away,' he said. 'I'm a stowaway.' He tried to continue but he couldn't keep it up. He let the puppet drop to his knee, his fingers still working the little lips like a goldfish left in the bottom of a basket. Finally he found the words.

'My father was killed by a mortar shell,' he said, 'in the fighting. Then my mother died. She drowned.' He said the next bit hesitantly. 'They put me in an orphanage. A terrible place. I ran away. I want to get to the New Land. Sunshine, steaks and … someone, anyone, who …' He searched for the words. '… knows my name.'

Max sat next to him holding up the red puppet as if it was listening. His eyes were glassy.

'You don't understand, do you?' mumbled Anton.

Max's nose was running and he sniffed loudly. He reached over with his free hand and patted Anton on the knee.

'No, he doesn't,' said a voice. 'But I do.'

Anton looked up and saw Max's mother standing at the open bathroom door with wet hair. She was dressed in a woolly dressing gown.

At that moment there were three loud knocks on the door.

Five

The two boys were alone in the house, something that rarely happened. Although the twins were now fourteen years old, their mother would not normally go out and leave them by themselves at night. But even though most of the fighting was over, the refuge where she worked still had emergencies.

And the power was out again. The whole town was in darkness.

'I'll come back as quickly as I can,' she said to Christopher. 'I know you'll look after Max until I'm back.'

'Do I have to sleep in his room?' said Christopher. 'He snores.'

'Yes, dear, you do. If he wakes up and one of us is not there he gets upset. And I need you to make sure his candle is out when he falls asleep. And that goes for you too.'

Christopher groaned and picked up the two puppets. 'More puppet talk?'

'More puppet talk,' she said with a smile. 'You know he loves it.'

* * *

As it turned out, the mother did not return until the early hours of the morning.

And when she did the boys were not there.

'I'm so sorry,' said the fire chief as they stared at the smouldering remains of the house. 'But only one of them survived.'

She stared with wide eyes, trying to make sense of it. Then her legs gave way and she dropped to the floor like an empty sack

'No, no, no,' she sobbed.

'The other one's okay,' said the chief. 'He's in hospital for observation. Sedated. But I'm so sorry we couldn't save his brother. Everything was ablaze.'

The frantic mother rushed to the hospital ward and looked at her son sleeping soundly. Both puppets were on the pillow next to him. Tears started to fill her eyes. There was no way he would have parted from the puppets.

She gently kissed him on the forehead. 'Max, Max, Max,' she said gently. 'Oh, my love. You're alive.'

He opened his eyes and stared around the tiny room, confused.

'Oh, Max,' she said again. 'Thank God they saved you.'

His eyes were sleepy and half closed. He blinked and confusion showed in his eyes.

'Are okay,' he said.

'Oh, Max, my darling,' she sobbed. 'What would I have done if I'd lost you?'

'Lost you,' he repeated. He fumbled with the little green puppet and put it on a shaking hand. Then he moved its lips.

'Where Christopher, where Christopher?' he said.

'Christopher, Christopher, Christopher,' she repeated. Unbearable thoughts filled her mind. The burning house. The choking smoke. The heat. The flames. And her son in the middle of it. She opened her mouth but could only utter a despairing groan.

Finally she managed to say, 'Don't worry, sweetheart. Everything will be all right.'

He closed his eyes and let his hand fall over the side of the bed. The little green puppet fell to the floor.

'Christopher gone,' he mumbled sleepily. 'Christopher gone.'

Six

Anton's mind was in a muddle. But he was still alert enough to know what the three knocks meant. The game was up. He was caught. Max's mother would report him as a stowaway.

What did they do with stowaways? He'd heard stories about it. Bread and water, locked up in a cell and then handed over to the police at the first port.

Another three knocks demanded a response. Max's mother opened the door to reveal the man who had found Anton on the deck.

'It's about your boy,' he said. 'He was alone on the deck in the dark. In bad weather on the first night. You can't let them wander like that.'

'I'm sorry, officer,' she said. 'It won't happen again.'

'I'm not an officer,' he said. 'I'm a steward on Deck A.'

'Well, we appreciate your trouble,' she said. She went over to the bed and fetched a purse. She selected two notes and held them out. The steward looked at her disapprovingly. But he took the money and headed back down the corridor without another word.

Anton's head began to spin. What was going on? Why hadn't she handed him over? Why did she act as if he belonged here?

Max's mother waited until the steward was out of sight and then shut the door.

She regarded Anton silently and gave him a sad smile.

He noticed her black dress draped across the bed. And Max's jumper with the labels and the black armband. From somewhere deep inside he could feel the clamouring of questions that could not be asked.

'Well,' she said in a kindly voice. 'You must be ready for bed too.' She opened her suitcase and handed him a towel and a pair of Max's pyjamas. 'But first dry yourself and put these on.'

Anton went to the bathroom and changed.

When he returned, the woman turned to Max and pointed to the top bunk. He groaned in protest.

'Bed,' she said. 'Now.'

Max climbed into the bunk and screwed his eyes tightly closed.

'I am asleep,' he said.

His mother gave another sad smile. She reached into her bag and gave Anton a small package wrapped in newspaper.

'Here,' she said. 'Eat this. Then sleep.'

She went back into the bathroom and closed the door. Anton feverishly tore open the paper and started to shove small pieces of cold chicken into his mouth.

When it was finished he lay back and closed his eyes. A little later he heard the woman come out of the bathroom. By now Max was breathing heavily. Anton could tell by the regular sound that the boy really was asleep.

Anton lay there with one arm across his chest, the green puppet on the pillow next to him. He kept his eyes closed. He didn't want to answer any questions the woman might ask. He heard her bed squeak and then a click as she turned off the light.

The motion of the ship was now rhythmic like the gentle swing of a cradle. And, although he did not believe its promise of peaceful slumber, the movement was comforting and he allowed himself to fall into a deep and dreamless sleep.

*　*　*

In the morning, the woman gave both boys a shake. She was already dressed for the day.

'Come on, sleepyheads,' she said. 'Time for breakfast. Hurry up or we'll be late for the last sitting.'

Both boys quickly dressed. Max was jumping up and down and waving the red puppet. 'Christopher, Christopher, Christopher,' he yelled.

'No,' said his mother. 'This is Anton. Christopher has gone. Anton is your new friend.'

'New friend, Anton, Anton, nice boy, nice boy,' said Max.

Anton went through the motions of dressing and washing his face as if in a dream. Why hadn't she dragged him off to the captain as a stowaway? He wanted to say something but was frightened to break the spell that seemed to have fallen over him. He kept thinking that he would wake up and find himself back in Wolfdog Hall.

As they left the cabin Anton looked back. Max had tucked the green puppet into the bottom bunk. It seemed to be staring reproachfully at Anton and for some reason he felt guilty for going off without it.

They made their way along the narrow corridors and up a number of staircases. Max's mother stopped every now and then to check a map of the boat. She peered into a room with an open door where two women and a man were patching uniforms and tablecloths.

'I wonder if passengers can use this room,' she said. 'I like sewing.'

'Hungry,' said Max.

His mother pointed at a sign at the end of the corridor. 'There it is,' she said. 'Dining Room.'

The dining room was a large windowless room with fifty or so tables. They were all bolted to the floor. Families chattered excitedly after their first night at sea. Friendship groups were already forming as the emigrants chose seats next to people they had met the day before. Max's mother selected a quiet table in a corner.

She pointed to a blackboard where the limited offerings were scrawled in white chalk. Some of the items had been crossed out. 'We'd better hurry,' she said. 'Before everything's gone. What are you going to have, Anton?'

He looked bewildered and then saw crew members threading their way through the tables dispensing food from large trays.

'Salami and rolls,' he said.

When the food came, Anton shovelled it into his mouth as if he had never eaten before. Max's mother smiled. But still she said nothing of any importance. She merely commented on the meal and the bad manners of some children at the next table.

Finally, she said, 'Kids like that will pick on Max. They'll call him names: Chrome Dome,

Simple Simon and things like that. They'll follow him around and snatch his badges or his beanie. They'll laugh at his bald head and give him a hard time.'

Anton gave her a sympathetic glance.

'His brother Christopher would have looked out for him on the boat.' Her voice began to tremble. She took a deep breath and a few seconds to compose herself.

'He was killed in a fire,' she said. 'Max misses him. We were all ready to emigrate when it happened. Only a few weeks ago.'

Anton, gasped. 'That's terrible,' he said.

'Yes,' she replied. 'Some people said we shouldn't leave but we had already been chosen to go to the New Land. Some of the lucky few. It was our one and only chance.'

'Yes,' said Anton. 'If you've got a bad deal, get out of it. And move on.'

She stared at him thoughtfully. 'If only it

was as easy as that,' she said. She nodded at Max, who didn't seem interested in their conversation. He was eyeing a steward who was carrying a plate of sausages from table to table.

Anton knew she was right. The memory of his mother was raw inside him. It took time to get over something like that. If you ever did.

'Max needs someone to look out for him,' she said. 'And I need ... some space.'

'Sausage,' yelled Max. He held one aloft in his fingers. His mother gently took it from his hand and put it on the plate.

'Manners,' was all she said. Then she turned back to Anton.

'Now,' she said. 'You tell me your story. The whole story. The truth. Don't you have someone, somewhere who can look after you?'

So, Anton told her the truth. His father and two uncles had both been killed in the fighting. All of his mother's family had died when their street was bombed. And then, only two months ago she had drowned. She couldn't swim. He hadn't been there when it happened. No one had been there. They found her body washed up on the beach. He had no one. He told her about Wolfdog Hall.

'I'm never going back there,' he said. 'Never ever.'

She stared at him thoughtfully, saying nothing while Max demolished another sausage.

Finally she said, 'If I take you to the captain they will send you back where you came from on the first boat going the other way.'

He said nothing. He knew it was true.

The children at the next table had started to throw food at each other. Their parents didn't seem to mind. She nodded towards them. 'I can't have kids like that teasing him and calling him names. His brother used to protect him but now he's ... gone. He needs someone else to look out for him – especially around the other kids.'

Anton tried to make sense of what she was saying. It seemed impossible.

'Me?' he said finally.

'You seem a nice boy,' she said. 'He likes you. You're smart. And you're good with him. You don't treat him like he's ... simple.' She obviously found the word distasteful.

'If it works out, the arrangement could become permanent. When we get to the New Land, you could live with us.'

Anton could hardly believe what he was hearing. She was offering him a home. But what if Max didn't like him? Or what if he failed to protect him? What then? It would be off to an orphanage somewhere.

He stared at Max sitting there in a jumper covered in badges, happily wolfing down his food, the red puppet on the table next to him. Anton felt a warm glow of affection. He liked Max. They liked each other. It might just work.

But it was risky. If anything happened to Max on his watch he would be back where he started. The thought of another loss was unbearable. He would have to watch Max like a hawk.

Anton impulsively held out his hand.

'Deal,' he said.

Max's mother gave a little laugh and took the out-stretched hand.

'Deal,' she said. 'But please don't let me down.'

Max suddenly started to cackle excitedly.

'Deal,' he yelled. 'Deal, deal, deal.'

His mother looked at him in surprise but didn't respond.

'Okay,' she said to Anton. 'Go out and have some fun. Take him for a walk around the deck to explore the ship. And explain things to him. But don't let him near the railing. Or the swimming pool. He can't swim.'

'Can't swim,' mumbled Max.

Anton grinned. 'That makes two of us, Max,' he said.

She stood up and patted her son on the head.

'Do what Anton tells you,' she said. Then, dropping her voice to a whisper she leaned down and spoke in Anton's ear. 'I need time alone. I have to pretend to be happy, for Max. But I also have to grieve for my lost son. I need room to cry.'

She blinked back tears and then added, 'So do you. I will make sure you have your own time, as well.'

She stood up and made her way across the dining room and was gone.

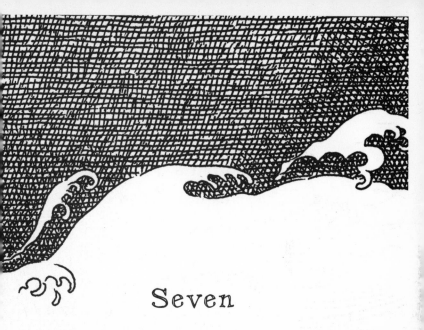

Seven

When the boys had finished every last morsel of their breakfast Anton said, 'Come on. Let's explore.'

'Let's 'plore,' said Max happily. He held up the little red puppet and pretended to make it talk.

'Nice Anton,' he squeaked.

They made their way up a staircase and emerged into bright sunlight. The sea was flat and blue and full of hope. But the ship was tired. Peeling paint and rust told a tale of neglect and wear. The crew had tried to disguise its history as a troop ship but its battle scars still showed.

Faded deckchairs and old sofas were being claimed by parents holding books and magazines. Children were playing deck quoits; some were eyeing the tiny swimming pool wondering if it would be warm enough yet.

The migrants were trying to adjust to their first taste of freedom and safety. Learning how to relax. Slowly putting aside the terrors that had come with them like unpacked luggage. A small group hung over the railings and stared at the flat sea as it swirled past.

Suddenly an excited cry went up.

'Dolphins, dolphins.'

The chairs were quickly deserted as the other passengers rushed to the railings.

Max rushed with them.

'Come back, come back,' shouted Anton. But he was too late. Max shoved his way through the jostling bodies and cried out excitedly. 'Sharks, sharks, sharks.'

'No, not sharks, dolphins,' said an old man.

Anton grabbed Max's hand and pulled. But the excited boy clung to the rail and refused to budge.

Anton groaned with despair. He had already failed in his first task and let Max rush to the railing. The boy's mother might even be in the crowd somewhere. He snatched a quick glance behind him but couldn't see her.

Soon the dolphins disappeared and the crowd dispersed. With a sinking heart Anton noticed a woman dressed all in black disappearing through a door. He couldn't be sure. It might have been her. She could have been following him to see if he was up to the task.

If she was watching, he would need to prove himself. But even if she wasn't, there was no way he would ever let Max come to any harm.

A group of children hurried past with their parents. One of them suddenly shouted out, 'There it is: Recreation Room.'

'Come on, Max,' said Anton. 'This is a safe place to start.'

They followed the group through the steel door into a dark, noisy room. There were small children in a sandpit and others playing with building blocks. One wall held a few tattered books and nearby were a number of tables where children were painting and drawing.

Max's eyes opened wide. He rushed to one of the drawing tables and snatched up a crayon. He scribbled excitedly and then thrust the piece of paper at Anton.

'What it say?' he yelled. 'What it say?'

Anton received the words like an angry slap to the face.

'Rubbish,' he snapped out.

He saw the look of surprise and bewilderment on Max's face.

'Sorry,' he said. 'Sorry. I don't know why I said that.' He took the piece of paper and pretended to read it. 'It says, "Max is very clever".'

Max beamed.

Anton was glad that Max's mother had not overheard that exchange. She would have found it hard to forgive him.

He took Max's hand and led him back out onto the deck. 'I have to teach you a few things. So that you are safe.'

'Are safe,' said Max. He pulled off his beanie and scratched his bald head.

At that moment a tall, good-looking boy passed them and mumbled.

'Dumb head.'

Max blinked in alarm.

'Don't take any notice,' said Anton. 'He thinks he knows more than you. But that's not what counts. You are kind. You are friendly. I might know more than you but that doesn't mean that I'm better than you. You took my hand and brought me onto this ship. You've given me a life. Imagine that.'

He stopped speaking. For a moment, he thought that Max was going to cry. But he just said, ''Magine that.'

'There's a lot I can teach you,' said Anton. 'Firstly, don't go near the railings. It's dangerous. And I will get into trouble if you do. If you fall over you'll ... drown.'

The word brought tears to his eyes. He tried unsuccessfully to blink back the memory of his dead mother.

Max was pointing to a lifebuoy that was roped to the railings.

Anton said, 'Those are to save people if they fall in. Lifebuoys.'

Max ran along the deck and pointed at another lifebuoy.

'Life girl?' he said.

Anton laughed.

'Good joke,' he said.

'Good joke,' yelled Max.

'There are also life jackets,' said Anton. 'You put them on if the ship is sinking. Let's go look.'

He said this loudly in case Max's mother was somewhere nearby. He wanted her to know that he was doing his job properly. Teaching Max about life jackets.

The two boys began to walk along the deck towards the back of the ship. Anton wondered where the life jackets might be stowed. It must be somewhere easy to find. In a cupboard. Or maybe in the lifeboats, which lined the lower deck. They walked further but he could find no sign of the elusive jackets.

He began to panic. Where were they? Where were the damned things?

Every time they passed a strolling group of passengers he checked to see if Max's mother was among them. But it was hard to tell – there were so many women dressed in black.

Anton continued to search for the ship's life jackets. He wanted to be able to report that he had taught Max how to use one. But he couldn't find them anywhere.

Suddenly the weather changed and a cool wind began to sweep the decks. Max clearly didn't like it. The labels on his jumper flapped and whipped around. Anton worried that one might get blown away and be lost in the ocean.

'We'll go to the back of the boat,' said Anton.

The back section of the lower deck was out of the wind and had a solid rail. A few people were leaning over it and staring down at the white froth stirred up by the propeller. The wind became stronger. Soon the two boys were alone, standing in the protection of the deck above. 'Let's sit down,' said Anton.

They perched on a long bench with a hinged lid, which ran along under the curtained windows of the deck cabins. They stared silently at the white trail that marked out the ship's journey through the heaving ocean. Anton was still worried about finding the life jackets. Quite clearly Max would not be able to even do up the buckles if the need arose.

Max held up the red puppet, which he had kept shoved up his jumper.

He put it on his hand and pretended that it was reading every word he saw written on the various signs on the ship. He rushed around from sign to sign. Each time he made the puppet say the same words, 'Max is very clever. Max is very clever.'

Anton sighed as the wind shifted direction and began to bite with frosty gusts.

He said, 'Don't tell your mum I couldn't find the life jackets.'

There was another gust of wind from the north. Max held up his little puppet. He moved the mouth. 'Cold,' he squeaked. 'Cold, cold, cold.'

His fingers and wrist were inside the red puppet. Its dress began to flap and then balloon out. The wind snatched at the puppet. In a flash, it was gone. Sucked over the back of the boat. Max gave a scream and ran to the railing.

'No, no, no,' yelled Anton.

They both stared down. The puppet was caught on a steel hook about an arm's length from the top of the rail. Max leaned over the rail and swiped desperately at the puppet.

Anton grabbed Max's trouser belt and pulled with all his might. Max fell backwards and skidded across the steel deck. He sat up and shook his head, confused.

Anton acted without thinking. He had to retrieve the puppet before Max tried again. Everything would be lost. Even if he didn't fall overboard, the kid would be inconsolable if he lost the puppet. Anton groaned. He had already let Max and his mother down. In less than an hour. The officer in the orphanage had been right. Life wasn't fair.

He leaned over and swiped at the puppet uselessly, just as Max had done. It was only slightly out of reach. The ocean beneath churned as the propeller thrashed and hummed. He stretched just a fraction more.

And then the world turned black.

Eight

It was a dream. It was a nightmare. He was in a dark, dark space. His mouth filled with salty water. It was bitterly cold. This couldn't be a dream – the agony was too real. And there was no waking moment of relief that follows a nightmare. The cold, wet truth that surrounded him told him where he was. He tried not to gasp for air but already his lungs were bursting. He thrashed wildly with his hands and kicked with his feet.

Suddenly his head burst through the surface. He coughed and spluttered and tried to blink away the stinging salt in his eyes.

He hadn't even been aware of falling. Just an agonising splat as he hit the water.

Anton tried to focus. Rolling waves rose around him like mountains, blocking off any chance of a distant view. He could see nothing but a world of water. An empty ocean surrounded him. He was just a head bobbing on the swell, which was about to relinquish him to the deep.

He coudn't see the ship. Desperate thoughts fought each other for attention. The ocean floor must be far beneath his feet. Nibbling crabs, sunken ships and their crews, sea snakes. An unbearable vision of his mother's body washing up onto the shore flitted through his head. Would he soon be joining her? Wasn't that the best thing? Just let go, just die. No, no, no. He wanted to live. And she would have wanted him to live.

He struggled and thrashed as the sea pulled him down for the second time. His movements were random, uncoordinated, futile, driven by panic. But once again his head broke the surface. He desperately sucked in the precious air. What did they say about drowning? The third time you went down was the last time you went down.

It seemed so senseless for his life to end like this. He was going to drown because he couldn't swim. Because he had never been taught the few simple movements that were needed to keep a body afloat.

His mind screamed for clarity. Was there any hope?

Think, think, think. Everything became an unintelligible buzz of blended nonsense. What had happened? Who knew that he had fallen overboard?

He was only minutes away from death. Terror

drove his thoughts. But then slower images began to take his attention.

He tried to clear his mind. All around he could see nothing but the blurry rise and fall of the sea and the wild clouds above. The ship, the ship. Where was the ship?

He sank again. Salty, cold, unforgiving water pulled him down, sucking his life, seeking to fill his bursting lungs.

And then. And then. Something brushed his arm. Rope. He was grasping a rope. He tried to pull himself up but the other end did not seem to be anchored in any way. Hand over hand he tried to climb to the surface but he was doing nothing but drag the rope down. Suddenly he felt it resist his pull.

Slowly he began to rise. His lungs were screaming for oxygen. He gave one last frantic heave on the rope and emerged into fresh air, gasping and spluttering.

The water chopped and splashed around his head. His cold, numb hands clung to the rope, which was attached to ... a lifebuoy.

Now his brain was really fuzzy. It didn't seem as if this could be true. Think, think, think. He had to get inside the thing before he sank again. Using his last reserves of strength he ducked down and emerged like a doll popping up through the hole of a doughnut. He draped both arms over the top of the supporting ring.

For an instant he felt relieved – but then all he could think of were his legs, dangling down like two tempting baits.

His right hand was throbbing. He examined his fingers. A trickle of blood was running down his thumb and onto his wrist. Sharks, sharks, sharks. Surely the water was too cold for sharks. But what if he was wrong? Sharks could smell blood from miles away, couldn't they?

A sound suddenly knocked the thought from his mind. At first he thought it must be a gull squawking. But when he heard it again, it sounded familiar. Like a word.

It was. Someone had seen his raised arm. There was another person in the water.

'Anton.'

He heard it again. 'Anton, Anton.' Someone was calling his name.

There was no mistake. He could see a figure swimming furiously towards him. He caught a glimpse of an orange life jacket and a bald head.

'Hang in there, Anton, I'm coming. I'm coming.'

Now the world really did start to slip away. Anton tried to untangle the hopes and fears that were fighting for his attention.

Voices in his head. And then a real voice.

'Fight it, man. Don't let go. Don't fall asleep. You can do this.'

It was Max. But it couldn't be. Now he knew that he was drowning. The last weird delusions of the doomed. He started to sink through the middle of the lifebuoy. The imaginary Max grabbed the trailing rope and wound it underneath Anton's arms. Then he deftly tied it to the edges of the lifebuoy.

'Stay awake,' yelled Max. 'Fight for your life.'

Suddenly a huge wall appeared. Bigger than any building Anton had ever seen.

He closed his eyes and slipped into another world.

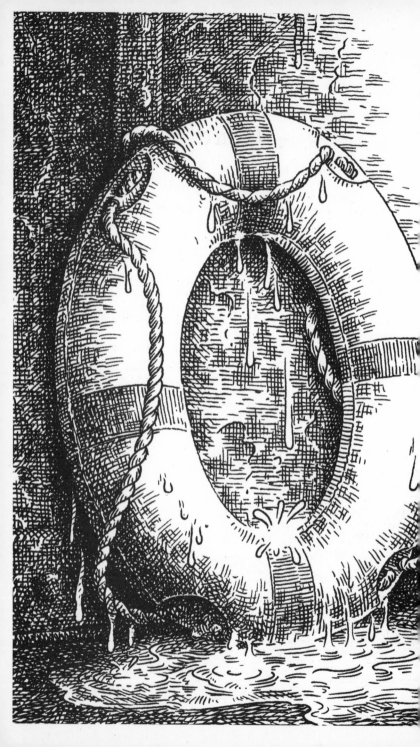

Nine

When he awoke Anton took a while to open his eyes. He was trying to make sense of it. Was he in this world or the next? Was he dreaming or dead?

He could sense that he was on a boat because of the gentle rise and fall of the floor as the vessel dug into the waves. And he knew that he was in a bed or a bunk because he was covered in blankets and had a pillow.

He was not alone either, because there was the gentle sound of breathing coming from above his head.

Finally, he opened his eyes and looked around. He immediately recognised the cabin. He could hear the water running in the bathroom and guessed that it must be Max's mother taking a morning shower.

Had it all been a dream? Falling into the sea? Yes, yes, yes. What a relief. He had another chance to look after Max properly. He was not going to be taken to the captain as a stowaway. He was still going to the land of plenty.

But then his joy vanished like water down a plughole.

A throbbing in his right hand confirmed that he was awake and in the real world. He examined his fingers and found a small white bandage tied around his thumb.

He remembered how he had held up his hand

so that the sharks wouldn't smell the blood in the water. The horror of it all began to return. He looked around in panic. There was a wet jumper on the small table and he could clearly see the two war medals that had been awarded posthumously to Max's father. Most of the ribbons and labels on it had been ruined by the water. There was no sign of the red puppet but the green one was right there in the bed, still staring at him with reproachful eyes.

Now he knew the terrible truth. It had not been a nightmare. He would not be staying in this warm and comfortable cabin for much longer. He really had let Max rush to the railing. And he himself had fallen into the ocean trying to recover the puppet.

This was the end of his journey to the New Land. Max's mother would never forgive him for letting her son run to the rail, let alone causing him to jump over the edge after him.

But something was wrong with all this. It was definitely dreamlike. Who had thrown in the lifebuoy? And had that really been Max coming to the rescue, saving his life?

A face appeared from the bunk above.

'Are you okay, Anton?'

It was Max, smiling down at him.

'I thought you were on your way to feeding the fishes at one stage there,' he said. 'But a very unlikely person came to the rescue.'

Anton stared at him in amazement.

'You?' he said.

'Sorry,' said Max. 'Forgive the boasting but my ego has taken a bit of a beating recently.' He climbed down from the top bunk and sat next to Anton.

At that moment, Max's mother emerged. She was dressed in a bright green cardigan and matching shirt.

She stood there silently, staring at the boys.

'We have to talk,' she said softly.

Anton found his voice.

'Who threw the lifebuoy to me?' he yelled. 'Was it really Max?'

'No,' she said.

'Who jumped in and saved me then? Was that Max?'

'No,' she answered.

'Who then?'

'Christopher,' she said. 'Christopher threw in the lifebuoy. And Christopher jumped in and saved you.'

Anton tried to make sense of her words. He stared at her in confusion.

'Christopher?' he yelled. 'He's dead.'

Anton looked at Max. Then he stared at the photograph on the table of the two identical brothers and his mind began to swirl.

She answered quickly. 'My other son died in the fire. But he wasn't who I thought he was.'

Her voice was close to breaking. She turned her attention to the boy on the top bunk.

'What happened in the burning house?' she croaked. 'What happened the night Max died?'

The boy climbed down and stood in the centre of the cabin. They both had their eyes locked onto him. Anton was still in a daze. The boy standing in front of him looked exactly like Max. But he was Christopher. It was Max who had died in the fire.

Christopher spoke frantically, blurring the words in his rush.

'It was my fault. I took both the puppets. I was sick of them. I wanted to sleep. Max kept running down to my room and waking me up with them. So I took them away from him and finally got some sleep. He must have knocked his candle over. I couldn't even get up the stairs to unlock his door. The whole place was on fire and I couldn't breathe. The flames spread like crazy.

The smoke was terrible. The fireman dragged me out just before the whole house collapsed. I passed out and that's all I remember. When I woke up I was in hospital and they told me that my brother was dead.'

Now his mother's voice was filled with agony and confusion.

'Why did you pretend to be Max? Why, why, why?'

Anton could tell that Christopher was struggling for the courage to say words he had never been able to utter. Then he spat them out like bullets.

'Because he was your favourite. Because he needed looking after. And it was my fault. I got all the blood when you were pregnant with us. You couldn't live without him. I knew that. When I opened my eyes in the hospital you thought I was him. You wanted it to be him. And you were so relieved it was him. I couldn't bear to see you collapse. You needed him more than you needed me.'

She began to sob. 'We both loved him,' she said, trembling. 'And I loved you both. I always loved you both. Why do you think I wanted to hide away here in the cabin? I needed space to grieve. For you. For you. I thought you were gone forever. And now we are both grieving for Max.'

'You don't understand,' said Christopher. 'It was still all my fault. I was supposed to look after him.'

'No, no, no,' she yelled. She suddenly threw her arms around him and squeezed and squeezed, not allowing him to say another word.

Anton said nothing. He was overwhelmed by the sad story unfolding in front of him. And he had his own grief and memories to deal with. The sight of Christopher's mother giving her son the comfort he so desperately needed plunged him into a personal pool of sorrow.

His own mother was gone forever. Still and lifeless in the ground of an unlucky land.

He began to cry himself.

Now they were all crying.

Christopher's mother stroked her son's cheek. 'I should never have let you look after him,' she said. 'It wasn't your responsibility. It was mine.' She put her arms around his shoulders, pulling him close.

'Nothing was your fault. That thing about the blood. Who told you about that?'

'Monochorionic twins. I looked it up last year in that medical dictionary you kept hidden on top of the kitchen cupboard.'

'Of course you did,' she replied. 'Nothing ever escaped you. That's your trouble. You know too much for your age.'

'You even had the page marked,' said Christopher.

Anton was staring at him in admiration.

A cloud of deep anguish passed across the woman's face and her voice trembled as she spoke.

'No child can feel responsible for what happened before they were born. I was tired of Max's puppet-talk as much as you. And the fire wasn't your fault. You did everything you could to save him. You were a marvellous brother to Max. And to pretend to be him after he died, just to help me cope, was an amazing thing to do. You are a hero.'

'Twice,' blurted out Anton excitedly. 'You are a hero twice. You saved me.'

She put her arms around both boys and hugged them so tightly that they could hardly breathe.

Then she spoke to Anton. 'I should never have given you the responsibility either. But when you came along I could see how much you liked each other. And Max would have had a real friend. I thought I could help you both.'

The room suddenly seemed warm. 'Let's go on deck,' she said.

'Good idea,' said Anton. And then he shyly added, 'Thanks, Pat.'

Ten

The sun was farewelling a golden sea as they made their way aft.

'What's going to happen to Anton now?' said Christopher.

'He's coming to the New Land to live with us, of course,' she said. 'If he wants to.'

'I want to,' said Anton.

'So do I,' said Christopher. 'I want it very much.'

'We will never forget Max,' she said. 'And Anton will never forget his mother and father. But in the end the pain will grow less. In the New Land, there is peace and food and forests. And the chance for a new beginning.' She put her arms around both boys. 'We are a family. We will look after each other.'

'Anton has already taught me a lot,' said Christopher. 'All about lifebuoys.'

'And life girls,' said Anton. He gave Christopher a friendly punch on the shoulder. Then he said, 'You should be teaching me how to ...' His voice trailed off.

'I can and I will,' said Christopher.

His mother smiled. 'Swim?' she asked.

'No,' they both shouted at the same time.

She raised a questioning eyebrow.

'I'm good at hiding it,' said Anton. 'You thought I was reading the menu on the wall in the dining room. But really I was staring around to see what everyone else was eating.'

Her eyes widened as she understood. Then she said, 'You're right. Christopher can teach you. And so can I.'

They stared silently at the white trail that marked out the ship's journey through the choppy ocean. Then they perched on the long bench with a hinged lid that ran along under the curtained windows of the deck cabins.

The bench with the words LIFE JACKETS written clearly on the top in large black letters.

Paul Jennings has written over one hundred
stories and has won every Australian children's choice
book award. Since the publication of *Unreal!* in 1985,
readers all around the world have loved his books.
The top-rating TV series *Round the Twist* was based
on a selection of his enormously popular short-story
collections such as *Unseen!* In 1995 he was made a
Member of the Order of Australia for services
to children's literature and he was awarded
the prestigious Dromkeen Medal in 2001.

A Different Boy is the second Paul Jennings title to
be published in the UK by Old Barn Books, after
A Different Dog, and is very loosely based on Paul's
experience of emigrating to Australia from England
as a child. He is currently working on a third,
connected, title, *A Different Land*.

www.pauljennings.com.au